# Hansel & Gretel

## Book & Lyrics by
## Kristin Walter

## Music by
## Michael Walter
## and Karen Biscopink

Baker's Plays
7611 Sunset Blvd.
Los Angeles, CA 90042
BAKERSPLAYS.COM

*HANSEL AND GRETEL* was first produced in April, 2008 at Manhattan Children's Theatre. The production was directed by Bruce Merrill, with musical direction by Nathan Atkinson and set design by Cully Long. The cast was as follows:

**HANK**................................................................Gilbert  Molina
**GERTIE**.................................................................Julia Hochner
**MOTHER**.........................................................Kelslan  Scarbrough
**FATHER**....................................................................Alvin Chan
**WITCH**....................................................................Rori Nogee

## RENTAL MATERIALS

An orchestration consisting of **Piano/Vocal Scores** will be loaned two months prior to the production ONLY on the receipt of the Licensing Fee quoted for all performances, the rental fee and a refundable deposit.

Please contact Baker's Plays for perusal of the music materials as well as a performance license application.

# CHARACTERS

Hank

Gertie

Mother

Father

Witch

Boy

Girl

# SETTING

The play takes place in a cottage deep in the Appalachian mountains, the woods nearby, and in the Witch's gingerbread house.

# MUSICAL NUMBERS

*Grace* (**HANK, GERTIE, MOTHER, FATHER**)

*The Witch's Song* (**WITCH**)

*The Lord Will Lead Us Home* (**GERTIE, HANK**)

*The Candy Cottage* (**BOY, GIRL**)

*Take Me Home* (**GERTIE, HANK**)

*Grace (Reprise)* (**HANK, GERTIE, MOTHER, FATHER**)

# Scene One

*(The main room of a small cottage. A family of four is sitting around the dinner table. There is a plate in the center covered with a tea towel. They are singing Grace.)*

**SONG - GRACE**

**ALL.**
> LORD OF THE MOUNTAINS
> LORD OF THE TREES
> LORD OF THE POSSUMS
> AND LORD OF THE BEES
> WE GATHER TOGETHER
> AT THE END OF THE DAY
> TO OFFER THIS BLESSING
> TO HIM THAT WE PRAY.
> THANK YOU FOR SHINING
> THE SUN IN THE SKY
> THANKS FOR THE STARS
> O'ER THE BED WHERE I LIE
> THANKS FOR ALL BIRDS
> AND THANKS FOR EACH BEAST
> BUT WE'RE MOST GRATEFUL, LORD
> FOR THIS BOUNTIFUL FEAST.

**MAMA.** *(removing towel to reveal four small pieces of bread)* I reckon it ain't much of a feast.

**HANK.** I don't know what you mean, Mama.

**DADDY.** *(biting into a piece of bread)* Why, we're eatin' high on the hog this season!

**MAMA.** I just wish we had some hog, or some taters even.

**HANK.** Don't fret none, Mama. I'm as full as a tick from lunch.

**GERTIE.** I couldn't eat another bite.

**MAMA.** I could see the bottom of the flour barrel this morning. We only got enough for a couple more days.

**DADDY.** I'll go back to the mine in the morning. I heard some men talkin' this afternoon – they said there might be some work this week.

**MAMA.** I'll go out and check the traps tomorrow. We might a caught us a squirrel or two.

**HANK.** Or a rabbit.

**GERTIE.** Rabbit stew!

**HANK.** Rabbit stew's my favorite!

**GERTIE.** Hank and I can go pick some berries. There're still a heap of 'em on the bushes by the creek.

**MAMA.** If the bears ain't got to 'em first.

**GERTIE.** Oh, Mama, there ain't no bears out here.

**DADDY.** Well then, the wolves might-a eaten' 'em all up.

**HANK.** There ain't no wolves neither.

**MAMA.** Well, maybe the witch took 'em to make her sugar house.

**GERTIE.** Sugar house?

**HANK.** What sugar house?

**GERTIE.** What witch?

**DADDY.** Don't tell me you ain't never heard of Hansel and Gretel!

**HANK.** Who?

**DADDY.** Hansel and Gretel. My Granny used to spin this yarn for me when I was no bigger than the two of you.

**HANK.** Tell us!

**GERTIE.** You tell the best stories!

**DADDY.** Well, let me get my pipe…

**MAMA.** We ain't had no tobacco in two years, why do you hang on to that pipe?

**DADDY.** Hush up, Mama and quit pesterin' me. It's my storytellin' pipe. *(puts it in his mouth)* Now, don't that make me look like a proper storyteller?

**GERTIE.** It's just the thing, Daddy. Now tell us about Hansel and Gretel.

**DADDY.** Mama, you comin'?

**MAMA.** Oh, I wouldn't miss it. Scootch over, you two and give me a little piece of floor.

**DADDY.** You settled?

**MAMA.** Pay me no mind – you just tell your story, Mr. Storyteller man.

**DADDY.** I reckon I will. Once upon a time, there were two little children by the names of Hansel and Gretel. They were brother and sister, and they were very poor.

**HANK.** Like us!

**DADDY.** A little like you. Their folks was out of work and they didn't get much food to eat. Some days, they didn't even get bread. Those poor little kids was so skinny a good puff a wind would've blown 'em away.

**GERTIE.** Poor little Hansel and Gretel. Didn't they have berries to pick or fish to catch?

**DADDY.** Nope. They was hungry and cold all the dad gum time.

**HANK.** Well, at least they had their Mama and Daddy.

**DADDY.** Well, they had their Daddy, who loved them very much. But their Mama was a mean as a snake, and jest about as ugly.

**MAMA.** Oh, fer cryin' out loud!

**DADDY.** Hush up. I'm telling a story here. One night, their Mama decided they couldn't take care of those kids any more. So she led 'em off into the forest and she left 'em there.

**GERTIE.** That's just the worst story I ever heard!

**HANK.** Did they die?

**DADDY.** They sure didn't. Because Hansel was smart. They were goin' so far into the woods, he wasn't so sure his Mama knew the way back, so he left a trail of breadcrumbs so they could find their way back home.

**HANK.** Hansel wasn't no dummy, was he?

**GERTIE.** So they followed the trail and ended up safe at home, where their Daddy was so happy to see them and…

**MAMA.** Hang on there, Gertie. Don't let's get ahead of ourselves here. You see, the birds up in the trees saw all those breadcrumbs, and they looked might tasty. So they swooped down and ate 'em all up.

**GERTIE.** Poor Hansel and Gretel! All alone in the forest!

**HANK.** What did they do then?

**MAMA.** Well, they started to walk in the direction they thought was home, but it wasn't. And it led them deeper and deeper into the dark woods.

**GERTIE.** I got the heebie jeebies.

**DADDY.** But then they came to a clearing. And in that clearing, was a house.

**GERTIE.** Was it their house?

**HANK.** Were they home?

**MAMA.** It wasn't their house. In fact, it was house the likes of which they'd never seen. It was all made of sugar!

**GERTIE.** A house made of sugar?

**MAMA.** The walls were made of gingerbread, and the roof was all vanilla icing. The windowpanes were made of meringue and the fenceposts were peppermint sticks!

**GERTIE.** Whose house was it? Was it a kindly old widow woman?

**HANK.** Was it a baker?

**DADDY.** It wasn't neither of those things.

**GERTIE.** I know! I know whose house it was! It was the witch!

**DADDY.** That's right, Gertie! It was a witch!

**HANK.** Was it a mean witch?

**DADDY.** It was such a mean witch!

**GERTIE.** Was it an ugly witch?

**MAMA.** This witch had fallen out of the ugly tree and hit every branch on the way down!

**GERTIE.** Well, if she was so mean and ugly, what was she doin' with such a beautiful and tasty house?

**DADDY.** She used that house to trap little children.

**HANK.** Now I got the heebie jeebies!

**GERTIE.** What did she do with the children once she'd trapped 'em?

**HANK.** Did she eat them?

**MAMA.** You'll just have to wait until tomorrow night to find out. Bedtime!

**HANK.** Mama, no!

**GERTIE.** Not now!

**MAMA.** Off to bed with you. You've got a big day of berry picking ahead of you. You wouldn't want to be too tired, now would you?

**GERTIE.** But I'll never get to sleep if I don't know how the story ends. I'll just be fannin' the covers all night!

**MAMA.** Just lay down and close your eyes. Now scoot!

**HANK.** Night, Mama. Night, Daddy.

**DADDY.** See you in the morning.

(**HANK** *and* **GERTIE** *exit.*)

**DADDY.** Now that was downright mean, sendin them off to bed without an ending to the story.

**MAMA.** It'll give them something to think about – get their minds off their empty bellies.

**DADDY.** Sure, they'll just be dreamin about cakes and cookies all night.

**MAMA.** Well, it's better than dreamin' about hard bread and water.

**DADDY.** When I get work again, we'll be eatin' gingerbread every night.

**MAMA.** You'll find something soon. You've just been down on your luck.

**DADDY.** Bad luck's the only kind of luck I've had lately. It was raining soup, I'd be caught with a fork.

**MAMA.** It'll get better soon. Everyone's been hit hard. Light that lamp, will you?

**DADDY.** I heard Charlie Wilson talking in town today.

**MAMA.** Could you hand me those dishes? Gotta get this kitchen cleaned up before we run out of coal oil.

**DADDY.** The mine company's still looking to explore the smaller shafts.

**MAMA.** No.

**DADDY.** The pay's real good.

**MAMA.** No. We've talked about this, and I won't do it. I won't send my children down into no mine shaft.

**DADDY.** I know.

**MAMA.** Little Jimmy Johnson near choked to death last spring.

**DADDY.** I know.

**MAMA.** What did you tell Charlie?

**DADDY.** That if he's fool enough to send his own kids down in that cave, he can go right on ahead. Hank and Gertie are gonna stay safe above ground.

**MAMA.** Good. We'll make it work somehow.

**DADDY.** *(smiles)* I suppose we can always take them out into the woods and leave them there.

**MAMA.** Maybe they'll find a gingerbread house and live happily ever after.

**DADDY.** They'd have to kill the witch first, though. And I hear she's a mean, ugly old thing.

**MAMA.** *(laughing)* Dishes are done. Let's get to bed ourselves. Long day tomorrow.

## Scene Two

*(The woods.* **HANK** *and* **GERTIE** *are picking berries off a bush.)*

**HANK.** Ain't these just the tastiest things?!

**GERTIE.** If you don't stop eating 'em, there'll be none left for Mama and Daddy.

**HANK.** Maybe Mama can bake a pie!

**GERTIE.** You need sugar to bake a pie, Hank, and we ain't got any of that.

**HANK.** Sugar! That's just like the story Daddy told us last night. A whole house made of nothing but sugar!

**GERTIE.** Just imagine it – gingerbread walls and icing and peppermint sticks – sounds like a big slice of heaven to me.

**HANK.** I dunno – it would get awful soggy when it rained.

**GERTIE.** Ah, shoot, Hank. It's a magic cottage. Ain't no rain can get inside a magic cottage.

**HANK.** How about snow?

**GERTIE.** Nope!

**HANK.** Hail? That would make an awful dent in the frosting.

**GERTIE.** Hey! I got an idea! Let's play a game!

**HANK.** What kind of a game?

**GERTIE.** Let's pretend that this bush is the cottage, and you and me are Hansel and Gretel.

**HANK.** Can I be Hansel?

**GERTIE.** Well, Hansel's the boy, ain't he? Come on! *(acting it out)* Oh, Hansel, I'm so hungry from all that walkin'.

**HANK.** Me too, Gretel. I sure do wish our Mama and Daddy hadn't gone and left us all by our lonesome out here in the dark woods. *(out of character)* How's that?

**GERTIE.** *(out of character)* That's mighty fine pretendin', Hank. *(in character)* Oooh, look Hansel! Over yonder! It's a gingerbread cottage!

**HANK.** I'm going to take a big bite out of it.

**GERTIE.** Wait a second, Hansel. We don't know who lives here.

**HANK.** *(out of character)* Sure we do, it's a mean, nasty…

**GERTIE.** But *we* don't know that yet.

**HANK.** Oh, right! *(in character)* I wonder who would live in such a house made all of sugar. Maybe it's a beautiful princess.

**GERTIE.** Or it might be a mean…

**HANK.** Nasty…

**GERTIE.** Ugly…

*(The **WITCH** pops up from behind the bush. The children scream and run back.)*

**HANK & GERTIE.** It's the witch! It's the witch!

**WITCH.** Now y'all just quit yer catterwallin'! You'll put me in a right state!

**GERTIE.** You scared us!

**HANK.** What're you doing, popping out at us like that? I done got goose bumps all over!

**WITCH.** Ain't meanin' to scare you. I'm just out doing a little berry pickin'.

**GERTIE.** Where do you live?

**WITCH.** Over yonder. Other side of the river.

**HANK.** How come we ain't never seen you before?

**WITCH.** I keep to myself mostly.

**GERTIE.** What are you doing all the way out here?

**WITCH.** Well ain't you two full of questions? How about you let me ask one or two?

**GERTIE.** Go ahead, then.

**WITCH.** Where's your house?

**HANK.** In the meadow back that way.

**WITCH.** What are you doin' all the way out here?

**GERTIE.** Berry pickin'.

**WITCH.** From the looks of you two, I'd guess that berries is all you been eatin'. You're so skinny a good puff of wind would blow you away.

**GERTIE.** *(a little defensive)* We had some bread for supper last night.

**HANK.** And Mama says there might be a rabbit in the traps today.

**WITCH.** Well, if your Mama says so, I guess it's true. Well, it was nice to meet you Hansel and Gretel.

**GERTIE.** Those ain't our names. I'm Gertie and that's Hank.

**WITCH.** Hogwash! I heard you before. You were callin' each other Hansel and Gretel.

**HANK.** We was just pretendin'.

**WITCH.** Pretendin' what?

**GERTIE.** Mama and Daddy told us a story last night before bedtime, and we was just make believing it was real.

**HANK.** Ain't you never heard of Hansel and Gretel?

**WITCH.** I guess I ain't.

**HANK.** Well, shucks, it's an awful good story. Hansel and Gretel's parents leave them all alone in the woods cuz they ain't got no money and can't feed 'em no more. So they walk and walk until they find a cottage made all of gingerbread.

**GERTIE.** It has icing for a roof and peppermint sticks for fenceposts.

**HANK.** They start to eat some of it, but then they're caught by the mean old witch who lives there.

**WITCH.** Well don't stop now. How does the story end?

**GERTIE.** Don't know. Daddy's gonna tell us the ending after supper tonight.

**WITCH.** Well, ain't that a shame. Sounded like a mighty fine tale.

**GERTIE.** Maybe if we run into you again, we'll tell you how it all works out.

**HANK.** I think the witch locks up Hansel and Gretel and eats 'em up.

**GERTIE.** Hank! Daddy's stories all have *happy* endings.

**WITCH.** I just bet they do. Well, off with you. You don't want to be late gettin' home now.

**GERTIE.** Right nice meetin' you, ma'am. *(They exit.)*

**WITCH.** The witch locks up Hansel and Gretel and eats 'em up. That sounds like a mighty happy ending to me. *(looks around)* This here's a pretty little valley. I reckon I could settle down here. Plenty of trees, good clean runnin' water, and a whole lot of folks ain't no one gonna miss. Startin' with little Hank and Gertie. Now let's see…a gingerbread house…I can make me a gingerbread house, that's the easy part. No, the trouble is gettin' their Mama and Daddy on my side. That calls for a mighty special curse. One that just works on the grownups. The kind that protect the children and are responsible for the children and tell the children dumb old things like never take candy from strangers. They spoil all my good fun! And I've got just the recipe. Good thing I still have some of that special ingredient in the cupboard. I'll whip up a big batch of gingerbread, and find that Mama near the rabbit traps. Then all I have to do is wait till the sun goes down!

***SONG - THE WITCH'S SONG***

**WITCH.** *(cont.)*

CHILDREN PLAYING LITTLE GAMES
WELL I CAN PLAY THEM TOO
I CAN SPIN A STORY
AND MAKE IT ALL COME TRUE

I CAN TRICK A MAMA
INTO GIVIN' UP HER YOUNG
THEN WORK DELICIOUS MAGIC
BEFORE THIS TUNE IS SUNG

YOU'D BETTER BEWARE
WHEN THE SUN GOES DOWN
YOU'D BETTER BEWARE
WITH A WITCH IN TOWN
I'LL EAT YOUR HEART AND SWALLOW YOUR SOULS
IN CAKES AND PIES AND JELLY ROLLS
SO TAKE CARE
WHEN THE SUN GOES DOWN

I CAN CURSE THE GROWN-UPS
I LEARNED FROM WITCHES PAST
ALL I NEED IS CHILDREN
AND MY SPELL'S AS GOOD AS CAST

I'LL MAKE A BATCH OF GINGERBREAD
SO TASTY AND SO FINE
ONE BITE OF IT AND MAMA'S
PRECIOUS CHILDREN WILL BE MINE

YOU'D BETTER BEWARE
WHEN THE SUN GOES DOWN
YOU'D BETTER BEWARE
WITH A WITCH IN TOWN

I'LL EAT YOUR HEART AND SWALLOW YOUR SOULS
IN CAKES AND PIES AND JELLY ROLLS
SO TAKE CARE
WHEN THE SUN GOES DOWN

## Scene Three

*(A clearing in the woods.* **MAMA** *is checking on the traps.)*

**MAMA.** *(sees a trap offstage)* Well thank the good Lord! We caught us a rabbit! Hank'll be so happy to have stew tonight. *(starts to exit)*

**WITCH.** *(enters)* I see you caught yourself a rabbit.

**MAMA.** *(jumps)* Oh! You startled me right out of my boots! I didn't see you there.

**WITCH.** Beg your pardon, ma'am. I'm awful sorry.

**MAMA.** My heart is racing just a mile a minute.

**WITCH.** Set down here and catch your breath. You're as white as a sheet.

**MAMA.** Thank you. *(She sits on a log.)*

**WITCH.** Did I hear you say somethin' about making a stew for Hank?

**MAMA.** I did.

**WITCH.** You wouldn't be talkin' about Hank and Gertie, would you?

**MAMA.** How do you know Hank and Gertie?

**WITCH.** I bumped into 'em pickin' berries over to the creek. You got yourself a mighty fine pair of youngsters.

**MAMA.** Thank you. They're good kids. We're real proud of 'em.

**WITCH.** Well, you should get that rabbit home.

**MAMA.** I should. *(starts to leave, then turns back)* It's a big rabbit – there'll be plenty of stew if you want to join us for supper.

**WITCH.** Oh, that is so very kind of you, but I gotta be on my way. *(turns to go, then turns back)* Do you think you might like a little gingerbread to bring home with you?

MAMA. I beg your pardon?

WITCH. Gingerbread. I made up a batch this afternoon and it's too much for one old lady to eat. I would have given it to the children, but they took off with their berries before I had the chance. Why don't you take it home for them? *(holds out a little parcel)*

MAMA. I ain't had gingerbread in a good five years. Lordy, that smells good.

WITCH. Have a bite.

MAMA. Oh, I couldn't. I'll just take it home for Hank and Gertie.

WITCH. *(brings out another small parcel)* Now look, here's a whole nother piece. There'll be plenty left for Hank and Gertie. Go on. Take a bite.

MAMA. It does look tasty. Maybe just a little nibble. *(takes a bite)* It's so good. *(takes another bite)* I ain't never had gingerbread this good. *(She eats the whole piece.)*

WITCH. Well, now look what you've done; you've gone and eaten it all up.

MAMA. *(She is changed – angry and demanding.)* You said there was more…Where is it?

WITCH. There's the other piece right here.

(**MAMA** *tries to grab it.*)

Now listen up. You take this piece home and give it straight to your husband. Don't let the children see it. Don't even let them know you've got it. This piece of gingerbread is just for their Daddy.

MAMA. Of course. Why would we waste good gingerbread on those little brats? Give it to me!

WITCH. Not yet. Tonight, you and your husband will take Hank and Gertie deep into the woods and you will leave them there.

MAMA. And then I can have more?

**WITCH.** And then you can have all the gingerbread your little heart desires. *(gives her the gingerbread)*

**MAMA.** *(grabs it)* All the gingerbread I want…

**WITCH.** Don't forget…

**MAMA.** Deep in the woods – I won't forget! *(exits)*

**WITCH.** Now that was just as easy as fallin' off a log.

*(**REPRISE**)*

### Scene Four

*(The table.* **MAMA** *is getting the rabbit stew ready.* **HANK** *and* **GERTIE** *run in.)*

**HANK.** Mama, we got berries!

**GERTIE.** Lots of berries! We filled a whole basket full.

**MAMA.** *(looking in the basket)* That ain't a whole basket. That's hardly none at all. What did you do, eat 'em all on the walk back?

**GERTIE.** We might have ate one or two, but…

**MAMA.** I sent you out to get enough berries for all of us!

**HANK.** But we did – look at how many…

**MAMA.** Your Daddy and me work all day long to get you enough to eat and you spend your day lollygaggin. *(throws the basket on the floor)*

**HANK.** The berries!

**GERTIE.** Mama! What is it? What's the matter?

**MAMA.** Ain't nothin' the matter with me. I'm gonna have me some rabbit stew for supper tonight. I just hope you filled your bellies with berries cuz that's all you're gonna get.

**HANK.** But you got rabbit…we were gonna have rabbit stew…

**MAMA.** Your Daddy and me will have rabbit stew. You get off to bed!

**GERTIE.** But Mama!

**MAMA.** Now! And Lord help you when your Daddy gets home!

*(***HANK** *and* **GERTIE** *run off crying.)*

**MAMA.** Come on, nighttime. I can't get rid of those brats fast enough.

**DADDY.** *(enters)* Do I hear cryin'? Are Gertie and Hank all right?

**MAMA.** I sent them to bed without supper.

**DADDY.** What would you do a thing like that for? And when we got rabbit, too!

**MAMA.** I sent them out to pick berries and they ate 'em all.

**DADDY.** Ain't these berries on the floor here?

**MAMA.** Not enough.

**DADDY.** Enough for what? What in the sam hill is the matter with you?

**MAMA.** I can't live this way anymore. There's no food, no money for nice things – and it's all their fault.

**DADDY.** Whose fault?

**MAMA.** Just think of it – twice as much bread at every meal...

**DADDY.** What are you sayin'?

**MAMA.** Tobacco for you, a new dress for me...

**DADDY.** I don't know what you mean.

**MAMA.** We can finally be free to do whatever we please...

**DADDY.** Mama! What has gotten into you?

**MAMA.** Gingerbread.

**DADDY.** Gingerbread?

**MAMA.** I met an old woman today. She gave me this. *(shows him the gingerbread)*

**DADDY.** *(still confused, but pleased)* Well ain't that just the nicest thing. And there's plenty for all of us.

**MAMA.** Plenty for both of us, you mean. Hank and Gertie don't get any.

**DADDY.** Of course they do. You just ain't feelin' yourself, Mama. I'm going to wake 'em up right now. We'll have ourselves some stew and...

**MAMA.** Wait! *(contrite)* You're right. I ain't myself today. I've been awful tired this past week, and I reckon I feel a chill comin' on.

**DADDY.** There's been a nasty flu around town this spring. You should go lay down.

**MAMA.** Oh, no need for that. I'll be fine. I just need a good hot meal with my family. I'll go wake the children. But first…you take a little bite.

**DADDY.** I think we should wait 'til after supper…

**MAMA.** Oh no, let's just have a little time just the two of us. Like it used to be. We don't get much time for just us these days. Go on, take a nibble.

**DADDY.** Well, all right. But just a little bite. *(takes a small bite, pauses then takes a much larger bite)* That's good gingerbread. *(eats the rest of the piece)* Out of my way. *(tries to leave)*

**MAMA.** Where are you goin'?

**DADDY.** I'm goin' out to find Charlie Wilson. There ain't no earthly reason that Hank and Gertie can't be earnin' their own way. They're small enough to fit in those mine shafts.

**MAMA.** Wait just a minute now. Even if they earn money, it'll still go just to feed them. I got myself a better idea. Why not get rid of 'em altogether?

**DADDY.** How do you mean?

**MAMA.** Let's take them out into the woods tonight. Deep into the woods, where they ain't got no chance of findin' their way back. And then let's leave 'em there.

**DADDY.** Well ain't you just as smart as a whip? They can make their own way in the world. They're nigh old enough.

**MAMA.** They can find their way to another town where no one knows them…

**DADDY.** Or us…

**MAMA.** And we ain't never gotta take care of 'em again.

**DADDY.** Well, if we've got a long walk ahead of us, why don't you dish out that stew?

**MAMA.** It'll be dark soon.

## Scene Five

*(The woods)*

**MAMA.** Hank! Gertie! Pick up your feet. We're in a hurry.

**GERTIE.** It's so dark out.

**HANK.** I'm awful sleepy.

**GERTIE.** Why did we have to wake up so early?

**DADDY.** We're checkin' the traps. Now hush up.

**GERTIE.** How come we're checkin' the traps in the middle of the night?

**MAMA.** I'm sick and tired of your foolish questions, Gertie. Now quit flappin' your gums and keep on movin'!

**GERTIE.** *(to* **HANK***)* We ain't got traps set out this far.

**HANK.** *(to* **GERTIE***)* There ain't nothin' out this far.

**DADDY.** Quit your chattering. We're here.

**HANK.** Where's here?

**MAMA.** You two just set there under that tree. Daddy and I are gonna go check the traps.

**GERTIE.** All right, Mama. *(They sit,* **PARENTS** *exit.)* Hank, what the devil is going on? Mama and Daddy never ball us out like that.

**HANK.** You reckon' maybe they're sick?

**GERTIE.** Might be. Or they could've gone plumb crazy. I can't figger.

**HANK.** Gertie, I'm scared. What if they don't never come back?

**GERTIE.** What do you mean, "if they don't never come back?" They're comin' back! They wouldn't just dump us in here the woods in the middle of the –

**HANK.** It's like the story! It's Hansel and Gretel! They're too poor to feed us, so they left us in the woods to die!

**GERTIE.** They wouldn't never do that! They won't even let us work in the mine, why would they leave us in the woods?

**HANK.** I don't know! They ain't been themselves all day. Mama's talkin' so mean, and Daddy yanked me out of bed so hard I darn near broke my arm.

**GERTIE.** We gotta find 'em. Which way did they go?

**HANK.** That way.

**GERTIE.** Then let's go. *(They begin to walk.)* Mama! Daddy!

**HANK.** Mama!

**GERTIE.** Daddy!

**HANK.** Where'd they go?!

**GERTIE.** Mama, Daddy, please come back! We'll be good, we promise!

**HANK.** We'll pick more berries –

**GERTIE.** We'll work in the mine if that'll help, just please don't leave us!

**HANK.** Mama!

**GERTIE.** They're gone, Hank.

**HANK.** They ain't gone! They can't be! Daddy!

**GERTIE.** They must've gotten lost. So we have to figger out what to do now.

**HANK.** I'm hungry.

**GERTIE.** I know. I'm hungry, too. Oh! Daddy gave us bread! *(pulls a small piece out of her pocket)* Get yours out, at least we can eat this.

**HANK.** I ain't got mine.

**GERTIE.** Where'd it go?

**HANK.** I ate it.

**GERTIE.** Already?

**HANK.** I was hungry. We didn't get no supper, remember?

**GERTIE.** Oh, Hank, look at you – you're a downright mess – crumbs all over your shirt and… *(They realize.)*

**GERTIE & HANK.** Breadcrumbs!

**GERTIE.** We can follow the trail!

**HANK.** And that'll lead us right back home!

*(They begin to search the ground for a breadcrumb trail.)*

**HANK.** I got some over here!

**GERTIE.** Well let's follow 'em. *(They walk for a moment.)* Where'd they go?

**HANK.** We must've lost the trail.

*(They search some more.)*

**GERTIE.** I found some over this way!

**HANK.** Well, come on, then! *(They walk for another moment.)* Trail's gone.

**GERTIE.** We're gettin' nowhere fast here, Hank.

**HANK.** Where're the crumbs? I ain't so tidy – I must of dropped darn near a thousand of 'em. *(brushing crumbs off his shirt – a bird whistles in the distance)*

**GERTIE.** The birds…Hank, remember in the story? The birds came down and ate all the crumbs so they couldn't find their way back.

**HANK.** *(sits down)* I'm tired.

**GERTIE.** Well we can't just give up. We gotta keep movin'.

**HANK.** Why? Mama and Daddy don't love us no more, we're all alone in the pitch dark. We might as well just stay here and let the bears get us.

**GERTIE.** Now you quit yer mopin' and get up off the ground. Mama and Daddy love us, they just got lost. We're gonna go find us some help.

**HANK.** You can go on – I ain't movin'.

**GERTIE.** Hank –

**HANK.** Quit pesterin' me. I'm tryin' to get some sleep.

**GERTIE.** I ain't leavin' without you.

**HANK.** I'm too tired.

**GERTIE.** You can do it, Hank. Just get up on your feet.

### SONG - *THE LORD WILL LEAD US HOME*

I KNOW YOU'RE FEELING FRIGHTENED
FAT FROM THOSE WE LOVE
I'LL COMFORT YOU WITH STRENGTH
THAT'S A BLESSING FROM ABOVE.
TAKE MY HAND AND PRAY
FOR THOSE WE HOLD SO DEAR
THOUGH THEY'RE LOST THEY'LL SOON BE FOUND
AND WE'LL HAVE NO MORE FEAR.

*(MUSICAL INTERLUDE)*

*(***GERTIE*** comforts **HANK** and they get ready to journey on.)*

**GERTIE & HANK.**

HOWEVER DARK IT FEELS OR
HOW FAR AWAY WE ROAM
THE STARS ARE SHINING BRIGHTLY
THE LORD WILL LEAD US HOME.

**HANK.** Sun's up. *(They begin walking.)*

**GERTIE.** Does any of this look familiar to you?

**HANK.** No. I ain't never been out here before.

**GERTIE.** Hey! Take a gander over there! Does that look like a clearing?

**HANK.** It does a little.

**GERTIE.** Well, where there's a clearing, there's sometimes a creek nearby.

**HANK.** Oh, I hope so! I'm so thirsty!

**GERTIE.** Maybe we can find a berry bush, too. *(She gasps as they enter the clearing. A gingerbread house is revealed. It's guarded by two gingerbread people.)* Land sakes! Will you take a look at that.

**HANK.** I got goosebumps.

**GERTIE.** My goosebumps have got goosebumps.

**HANK.** There really is a gingerbread house.

**GERTIE.** Gingerbread walls –

**HANK.** And an icing roof –

**GERTIE.** And fenceposts made of peppermint sticks!

**HANK.** Wait! What are those?

**GERTIE.** They look like giant gingerbread people.

**HANK.** It's a gingerbread boy and girl.

**GERTIE.** Do you reckon we could eat them?

**HANK.** I don't know. They look eatable. *(starts to walk over to them)*

**GERTIE.** Wait! Maybe this ain't such a good idea.

**HANK.** What do you mean?

**GERTIE.** Just think a minute, Hank. We got the rest of the story – Mama and Daddy lose us in the woods, birds eat up our breadcrumb trail and now we find us a big old gingerbread house. Don't you remember whose house it was?

**HANK.** I'm too hungry to think straight, Gertie. I'm takin' a bite of that cookie. *(starts to take a bite)*

**BOY.** Ouch!

**HANK.** *(to **GERTIE**)* What did you say?

**GERTIE.** I didn't say nothing.

**HANK.** You said, "ouch."

**GERTIE.** No, I didn't. But I still reckon it ain't such a good idea to -

*(**HANK** ignores her and goes in a second time.)*

**BOY.** Ouch!

**GERTIE.** Did you say "ouch?"

**HANK.** No. *(They back away from the **GINGERBREAD PEOPLE**.)* I think it was him.

**GERTIE.** Couldn't be. Could it?

(**GINGERBREAD PEOPLE** *begin to move.*)

***SONG - THE CANDY COTTAGE***

**BOY & GIRL.**

COME INTO THE CANDY COTTAGE
WE'VE GOT TREATS TO EAT
CUZ IN THIS HERE CANDY COTTAGE
EVERY TREAT IS SWEET

THERE'S PEPPERMINT AND LOLLIPOPS
AND LICORICE AND MORE
FANCY TASTES I'LL BET YOU
AIN'T NEVER HAD BEFORE

COME ON IN
JUST TASTE IT DON'T BE SHY
DIG RIGHT IN
DON'T KNOW UNTIL YOU TRY

THE GINGERBREAD IS TENDER
IT MELTS RIGHT ON YOUR TONGUE
THE PEPPERMINT IS CRUNCHY
BUT WAIT! WE'VE JUST BEGUN

BEFORE YOU EAT THE DOOR
CHEW ON A FROSTING COVERED WREATH
TOPPED WITH GUMMY GUMDROPS
THAT'LL STICK IN SIDE YOUR TEETH

THROUGH THE GATE
WHICH CANDY WILL YOU CHOOSE?
DON'T YOU WAIT
THERE AIN'T NO TIME TO LOSE

(*short dance break*)

WELCOME TO THE CANDY COTTAGE
COME AND FOLLOW ME
EAT UNTIL YOUR BELLIES BUST
AND BEST OF ALL IT'S FREE!

**BOY.** Welcome to the gingerbread cottage.

**GIRL.** Everything your heart desires, right here in the house.

**GERTIE.** *In* the house, or *on* the house?

**HANK.** Cuz my heart's desirin' a big piece of that wall.

**BOY.** You can have anything you want. Just come inside the gate.

**GERTIE.** Wait, Hank! Ain't you got a lick of sense?! We can't go in there!

**HANK.** Why on earth can't we?

**GERTIE.** There's a witch in there!

**HANK.** A witch?

**GERTIE.** Like in the story. Remember? A witch lived in the sugar house, and she…

**HANK.** She what? We never got to hear the rest of the story. I reckon she was a good witch. Ain't no bad witches gonna make a house like this.

**GERTIE.** What if it's a trap? And we're the rabbits?

**BOY.** Don't pay her no never mind, little boy. No one lives in this house.

**GIRL.** It was made just for little children to eat.

**BOY.** You come on in the gate.

**HANK.** See, Gertie. No one lives here. You're just yeller.

**GERTIE.** I ain't yeller, Hank.

**HANK.** You ain't got the backbone of a fish worm.

**GERTIE.** I ain't scared, I'm bein' careful. You wanna run in half cocked? Go ahead! I'm stayin' right here.

**HANK.** I will! *(He goes through the gate.)*

**BOY.** Yay! Welcome to the candy cottage! Eat some of that window!

**GIRL.** Try a piece of the door!

**HANK.** Oh! I never tasted anything so good in my whole life! Gertie, you gotta come in here!

**GIRL.** Come on, Gertie! Ain't nothing bad gonna happen.

**BOY.** Course not! Come on in!

**GERTIE.** There ain't no witch?

**GIRL & BOY.** There ain't no witch!

**HANK.** Quit bein' a scaredy cat. *(holds out a piece of gingerbread)* Try this. It melts right down in your mouth.

**GERTIE.** Well, I guess one bite can't kill me. *(She enters the gate and takes the piece.)* Oh, Hank, that's just about the best thing I ever ate. *(She goes to the door and takes a chunk out of it.)* I don't even care if there is a –

*(The **WITCH** enters through the door that **GERTIE** is eating.)*

**WITCH.** Who is eatin' my house?

*(The children scream.)*

**GERTIE.** It's the witch!

**HANK.** Run!

*(They try to run, but the **GINGERBREAD PEOPLE** grab them.)*

**BOY.** We told 'em not to eat any!

**GIRL.** We tried to keep 'em away, but they was just too strong!

**HANK.** That ain't true!

**GERTIE.** They said we could eat as much as we wanted! They said there wasn't no one who lived here!

**WITCH.** *(to the **GINGERBREAD PEOPLE**)* Now fess up, my little gingerbread children? Have you been telling these nice young'uns to eat my house?

**BOY.** No.

**GIRL.** We'd never do a thing like that.

**BOY.** Well maybe a little…

**GIRL.** But just this once.

**BOY.** They looked so hungry…

**HANK.** See! We told you!

**WITCH.** Now, don't you fret none, little boy. It's all hun-key-dorey.

**HANK.** You don't mind?

**WITCH.** Course not.

**GERTIE.** Wait a minute. We've seen you before. You're the old woman from the berry bushes.

**WITCH.** Well land sakes! I remember you now. What in tarnation are you doing all the way out here?

**GERTIE.** *(hesitates)* We got lost.

**WITCH.** Lost?

**HANK.** We got lost in the forest last night.

**WITCH.** What was you doing in the forest after dark?

**GERTIE.** We was walkin'.

**WITCH.** Walkin'? All by your lonesome?

**HANK.** Our mama and daddy was with us, but...

**WITCH.** But...

**GERTIE.** They got lost, too, we reckon', cuz they went off to check a squirrel trap and they didn't come back.

**GIRL.** Well, ain't that just terrible!

**BOY.** Do you reckon we should go look for 'em?

**WITCH.** Now you just hush up. I've seen this sort of thing before.

**GERTIE.** What sort of thing?

**WITCH.** When times get too tough on a family, some-times they just have to let the children make their own way in the world.

**GERTIE.** What do you mean?

**WITCH.** Does your daddy have himself a job?

**HANK.** He tries to get work, it's just hard right now.

**WITCH.** Can your mama feed you every day?

**GERTIE.** She can most days. Sometimes it's just the ber-ries that we pick.

**WITCH.** Oh, you poor little children. Your mama and daddy just can't take care of you no more. You was left out there in the woods.

**HANK.** That's a lie!

**GERTIE.** Our mama and daddy love us! They would never just leave us!

**WITCH.** Then why are you all the way out here? Your mama and daddy are safe at home while you wander through the forest.

**BOY.** That's lower than a snake's belly!

**GIRL.** That's rotten as a worm-eaten apple!

**HANK.** It's ain't true! It ain't! They never left us – I'll bet they're looking for us right now!

**WITCH.** Really? And were they acting queer yesterday? Did your mama holler at you?

**GERTIE.** How did you know about that?

**WITCH.** And did she send you to bed without no supper?

**GERTIE.** She did.

**WITCH.** And when your daddy come home, did he take her side?

**GERTIE.** He did.

**WITCH.** They ain't comin' to find you, little girl. You're on your own now.

**GERTIE.** Can you help us?

**BOY.** She sure can!

**GIRL.** She helps everyone!

**WITCH.** Come on inside. I got a big pot of stew on the stove. You still hungry?

**GERTIE.** I'm starved. Hank, you comin'?

**HANK.** What about the story, Gertie? What if she's a witch?

**GERTIE.** *(to the* **WITCH***)* That's right. We told you the story. How come you never said that you had a gingerbread house just like that one?

**WITCH.** I ain't gonna lie to you. I'm a witch.

*(They back away.)*

But there ain't nothing to be afeard of. I ain't gonna hurt you. I can make your dreams come true. You wanted to find a gingerbread house, didn't you?

**HANK.** I know I did.

**WITCH.** Well, there you have it. Your dreams came true. Now I think someone's dreaming about some stew.

**HANK.** What kind of stew?

**WITCH.** It's rabbit.

**HANK.** Rabbit? Really?

**WITCH.** Can't you smell it?

**HANK.** It sure smells good.

**WITCH.** Well, then, come on in.

**GERTIE.** I guess we know the ending to the story now.

**WITCH.** And it's a downright happy one.

(**GERTIE, HANK** *and* **WITCH** *exit into the cottage.*)

**BOY.** Those poor little chilluns. All alone in the great big world. It's a good thing they got Mother to help them now.

**GIRL.** Mother can fix anything. *(shivers)*

**BOY.** Someone walk over your grave?

**GIRL.** I've got a funny feeling. Almost like I've seen them kids somewhere.

**BOY.** That's queer. I got that feeling, too. But I can't quite put my finger on it. Do you reckon they've walked this way before?

**GIRL.** I don't think so. It ain't here that I remember 'em. If I close my eyes, I can see 'em in a field somewhere, in a cottage in a field, someplace far away.

**BOY.** But we ain't never been far away.

**GIRL.** I know. So why do I see 'em settin' at a wooden table, with a basket of bread and berries?

(**WITCH** *pokes her head out the door.*)

**WITCH.** You'd best be eating more of this. *(She hands them gingerbread.)*

**BOY.** Gingerbread!

**WITCH.** It's the special gingerbread. The kind I only make for you.

**GIRL.** Thank you, Mother. We love gingerbread. *(They eat.)* What were we saying?

**BOY.** We were saying that it's a good thing those children found this house. Mother'll help them, now.

**GIRL.** She sure will. Mother can fix anything. *(idea)* I know! *(to the* **WITCH***)* You should give *them* some of that special gingerbread.

**WITCH.** Oh, that won't help them. The special gingerbread don't work on children.

**BOY.** Good! That means there's more for us!

**WITCH.** And you can have all the special gingerbread you want. Any time you want it.

## Scene Six

*(Inside the gingerbread house.* **WITCH** *is stirring a big pot.)*

**WITCH.** Now you just set right down there and have yourselves a bowl of stew.

**GERTIE.** Thank you ma'am. You've been awful kind to us. I don't know how we can repay you.

**WITCH.** You can start by eatin' up that stew, and then you can help me with the bakin'.

**HANK.** Ain't you havin' any stew?

**WITCH.** I don't eat much rabbit.

**HANK.** What do you eat?

**WITCH.** You're full of questions, ain't you?

**GERTIE.** What are you bakin'?

**WITCH.** Well, it seems as though someone came out of the woods and ate up my shutters. So I guess I have to make some more.

**GERTIE.** But you're a witch. Can't you just wave a wand around and fix it up?

**WITCH.** Oh, it ain't quite that simple. I can cast a spell to make sure the gingerbread holds up in the rain, but I have to make it first.

**GERTIE.** Did you make the gingerbread people, too?

**WITCH.** I sure did. They help me around the place. Do you like them?

**GERTIE.** They're funny. Is it a spell that makes 'em talk?

**WITCH.** It's a simple enchantment.

**GERTIE.** Could you teach me? Maybe if I knew a few spells, we could find our way home. Your gingerbread people help you. Maybe I could make some that would help us.

**WITCH.** Well, now, let's see. *(She crosses to the door and lets the* **GINGERBREAD PEOPLE** *in.)* What do you think

WITCH. *(cont.)* about that? This little girl wants to learn a few spells to find her way home. Should we teach her?

GIRL. They want to go home?

BOY. But I don't want 'em to go home.

GIRL. I want 'em to stay and play with us!

*(They grab onto* GERTIE *and* HANK.*)*

You promised they'd stay and play with us!

HANK. Ouch!

GERTIE. You're hurtin' me! Please let go.

GIRL. I won't! I won't! I won't! You're gonna stay and play with me!

GERTIE. Please! Tell them to let us go!

WITCH. I don't think I can do that. You see, they only do what I want them to do. And I want you to stay right here.

GERTIE. But why?

WITCH. Oh, I have special plans for you two. *(to the* BOY*)* Get him into the cage! *(to the* GIRL*)* Lock the girl up in the pantry!

*(They drag* HANK *and* GERTIE.*)*

HANK. But you're a good witch!

GERTIE. You said we'd have a happy ending!

WITCH. I said there'd *be* a happy ending. I didn't say it would be yours. *(laughs)*

## Scene Seven

*(Inside the cottage. It's a month later and* **HANK** *is seated in the bottom of a cage.* **GERTIE** *is sweeping the floor.)*

**HANK.** Gertie?

**GERTIE.** Hush! She'll hear you!

**HANK.** How long have we been here?

**GERTIE.** By my count, it's been a month.

**HANK.** Why won't she let us go?

**GERTIE.** I don't know, Hank. She's a witch, ain't she? I don't reckon she's too kindhearted.

**HANK.** Do you reckon she did something awful to Mama and Daddy? Is that why they left us in the woods?

**GERTIE.** I don't know, Hank.

**HANK.** What's she going to do with us?

**GERTIE.** Keep us, I reckon. Like pets, or servants or some such.

**HANK.** I don't want to stay in this cage no more, Gertie. I want to go outside.

**GERTIE.** At least she feeds us. We're eating better than we ever have. Meat every single day, and good fresh bread.

**HANK.** I don't care. I'd rather have berries and Mama and Daddy than all the rabbit stew in the world.

**GERTIE.** Me, too.

*(The* **GINGERBREAD PEOPLE** *enter.)*

**BOY.** Are you *still* sweepin'?

**GIRL.** Mother sent us in to check up on you.

**GERTIE.** I'm nearly done.

**GIRL.** Then she says you gotta wash the supper dishes, beat the rugs, scrub the floors and light the oven so she can bake more gingerbread.

**BOY.** All before bedtime.

**GERTIE.** I can't do all that before bedtime! It's nearly dark now!

**BOY.** That's too bad for you. Mother says if you don't do what we say, you won't get any supper tomorrow.

**GERTIE.** I don't care. I'm tired, and I'm lonely and I just wanna go home!

**GIRL.** You are home. This is where you live and he lives and we live. Mother takes care of us and we live here.

**GERTIE.** We don't live here! We have a house in a little field with a creek nearby, and we have a Mama and Daddy who love us and take care of us! They're out there somewhere, and I know they're looking for us!

### *SONG - TAKE ME HOME*

THERE'S A SMALL PATCH OF LAND
JUST EAST OF THE MOUNTAINS
WHERE A CROOKED OLD TREE STANDS THE LONG TEST
OF TIME
IT'S GOT A STRONG TRUNK
AND PLENTY OF BRANCHES
TO HOLD US UP TIGHT WHEN WE GO FOR A CLIMB

A CLEAR WINDY CREEK
RUNS NEXT TO A COTTAGE
WITH THREE ROOMS A CHIMNEY AND CLEAN WOODEN
FLOORS
A FAT IRON STOVE
CROUCHED DOWN IN THE CORNER
BELCHES OUT HEAT AS IT RUMBLES AND ROARS

SO TAKE US HOME BROTHER
WON'T YOU LET US BE FREE?
WE'LL DRINK FROM THE STREAM AND WE'LL CLIMB
THE OLD TREE
WE'LL LAUGH AND WE'LL PLAY AND WE'LL RUN FAR
AND WIDE
WITH MAMA AND DADDY RIGHT BY OUR SIDE

**HANK.**

> I'LL SIP FROM MY CUP
> AND I'LL EAT FROM MY DISHES
> THE THICK RABBIT STEW MAMA COOKS UP JUST RIGHT
> AND WHEN I'M FILLED UP
> AND TIRED AND COZY
> I'LL CLIMB IN MY BED TO GET TUCKED IN SO TIGHT

**GERTIE & HANK.**

> WE'LL HAVE STORIES AND SINGIN'
> AND DANCIN' AND GAMES
> AND BERRIES, PLUMP JUICY AND RED
> BUT WE'LL NEVER NOT EVER AS LONG AS WE LIVE
> EAT ANOTHER BITE OF GINGERBREAD
>
> SO TAKE US HOME SISTER
> WON'T YOU LET US BE FREE?
> WE'LL DRINK FROM THE STREAM AND WE'LL CLIMB
> THE OLD TREE
> WE'LL LAUGH AND WE'LL PLAY AND WE'LL RUN FAR
> AND WIDE
> WITH MAMA AND DADDY RIGHT BY OUR SIDE.

**BOY.** I know that house.

**GERTIE.** What?

**GIRL.** I know it, too. It's an old house, with shingles on the roof and a water pump out back.

**BOY.** With a blue handle. The pump has a blue handle.

**HANK.** How did you know that?

**GERTIE.** Have you been there?

**GIRL.** It feels like I have. Like I know that place.

> (**WITCH** *enters.*)

**WITCH.** This looks like a cozy little scene. What's going on in here?

**GERTIE.** Nothin'! I was just finishin' the sweepin'. Then I'm gonna scrub the floors and beat the rugs and…

**GIRL.** Gertie was just tellin' us about her house.

**GERTIE.** No, I wasn't!

**WITCH.** Nonsense! Gertie ain't got a house. She lives right here with us.

**BOY.** But it seemed so familiar. It has shingles…

**GIRL.** And a water pump.

**WITCH.** I think my gingerbread children are getting hungry.

**GIRL.** Hungry?

**WITCH.** Don't you want another bite? *(She holds out a piece of gingerbread.)*

**BOY.** Oh, thank you Mother!

**GIRL.** I am hungry. *(They eat. She turns back to* **GERTIE.** *)* Are you going to stand there lollygaggin' all day? Finish the sweepin'!

**BOY.** And then do the rest of those chores or it'll be no supper for you tomorrow! *(They exit.)*

**HANK.** How'd they know about our house?

**WITCH.** Don't you pay them no mind. They're just a bit bumfuzzled. Best not to give it another thought. Now let me take a look at you.

**GERTIE.** Stay away from him!

**WITCH.** Well ain't you just full of vim and vigger? Don't you cross me, little girl. I'm just going to take a look at your brother. *(She goes to him.)* Hmmm… you're coming along nicely. All that good food agrees with you. Mother takes good care of you, don't she?

**HANK.** You're not my mother! And I don't want your dumb old food!

**WITCH.** Of course you do.

**GERTIE.** He says he don't want it! So you just stay away from him!

**WITCH.** You're going to tell me what to do, now?

**GERTIE.** Yes, I am! Mama and Daddy are gone and I'm the oldest, so I have to take care of Hank. And I will take care of him! I'll find a way out of here and I'll get us back home! You'll see!

**WITCH.** Well, you're all grown up now, ain't you? *(looks at the gingerbread in her hand – aside)* I reckon it's time for some of the special gingerbread. *(to* **GERTIE***)* I'm sorry, little Gertie. I know you want to look after your little brother. But right now, I know what's best for you both, and I need you to trust me. After all, your parents ain't around no more, and someone has to teach you right from wrong.

**GERTIE.** I know it's wrong to lock little boys up in cages and make their sisters work all day long.

**WITCH.** Poor little Gertie. I reckon you ain't been eating enough. Have some gingerbread.

**GERTIE.** I don't want none of your gingerbread. The whole house is made of it – I can have some any time I want.

**WITCH.** But this is my special gingerbread. It's tastier than the house. Take just a little – as a token of my thanks. You've been so helpful around the house this past month; I don't know what I would have done without you. Go on. Just a bite.

**GERTIE.** Fine. *(She takes the gingerbread, but she doesn't eat it.)*

**WITCH.** Be sure you eat that all up before bed. And you can save the rest of your chores until the morning. *(She exits.)*

**GERTIE.** I hate her!

**HANK.** Don't worry, Gertie. You don't have to take care of me.

**GERTIE.** Yes, I do. I'm older than you and I have to be the grown-up. We're lost and we're trapped and you're stuck in a cage and I have no cotton-pickin' idea how to get us out!

HANK. Hang in there, Gertie. we'll figure out some-thing. Besides, I'm the one got us in the mess, ain't I? If I hadn't been all fired up eager to eat some gingerbread, we would never have gone in the gate.

GERTIE. It ain't your fault, Hank. I wanted the story to have a happy ending, too.

HANK. It will have a happy ending. We'll make one. We'll bide our time and we'll make a plan and we'll get out of here. I promise.

GERTIE. Now *you* sound like the grown-up. Here. *(gives him the gingerbread)* I don't want it.

HANK. You sure? It's gingerbread.

GERTIE. I've had about all the gingerbread I can eat. Somehow it don't taste so good no more.

HANK. Well, if you ain't gonna eat it… *(He takes a small bite.)* Gosh dang, the witch was right…it is tastier than the house.

GERTIE. Maybe I will have a little bite then.

HANK. Get away! You said you didn't want none!

GERTIE. What?

HANK. You gave it up! Finders keepers losers weepers! And get away from my cage! Mother wouldn't like it if she saw you so close.

GERTIE. Mother? Hank, what's gotten into you?

HANK. You just stay away from me, Gertie!

GERTIE. But…

HANK. Stay away!

GERTIE. Give me that! *(She snatches the rest of the ginger-bread from him.)* Hank, it's Gertie. Listen to me.

HANK. I don't have to listen to you. You're not the boss of me no more! I only have to listen to Mother.

GERTIE. Hank, look at me. You're my brother. We live with Mama and Daddy in a little house with shingles and a water pump. We go out berry pickin' together and we make up stories, and…

**HANK.** Gertie? What's goin' on? My head's all fuzzy. I don't know why I was so mean to you just then. It was like I wasn't even myself.

**GERTIE.** The gingerbread! There's something wrong – it's enchanted somehow.

**HANK.** Enchanted?

**GERTIE.** Hank – do you know where the witch keeps the special gingerbread? The cookies that she gives the gingerbread people.

**HANK.** No – I've seen her bake it, but I don't know where she stores it. Why do you want to know?

**GERTIE.** I know how to get us out!

**HANK.** How?

**GERTIE.** I'm just gonna need a little help from the gingerbread people. Oh, Hank, it's going to work, I just know it!

## Scene Eight

*(The inside of the cottage.* **GERTIE** *is wrapping gingerbread in cloth. The* **GINGERBREAD PEOPLE** *enter.* **GERTIE** *hides what she's been doing.)*

**BOY.** It smells like cookies in here!

**GIRL.** Did Mother bake us the special gingerbread?

**GERTIE.** She did. She's been bakin' all night. You want some?

**BOY.** We always want gingerbread!

**GERTIE.** Well, ain't that a shame?

**BOY.** 'Smatter?

**GERTIE.** I don't know where it is.

**BOY.** Ah, shoot! I'm hungry.

**GERTIE.** Why don't you just tell me where it is?

**GIRL.** I'm ain't sure we're allowed to do that.

**GERTIE.** Why not? She's just going to give you some, anyways, so why don't we save her the trouble? Ain't you always saying that Mother works her fingers to the bone?

**BOY.** Poor Mother. I reckon we should help her out more. Gingerbread's in the highest cupboard on the highest shelf. Up there.

**GERTIE.** That's a high cupboard. I guess I can stand on this chair.

**HANK.** Be careful, Gertie!

**GIRL.** Oh, are you awake? *(She goes to his chair.)* Still stuck in the cage, are you?

**HANK.** So what if I am?

**GERTIE.** *(climbing on the chair)* Hank, be nice.

**GIRL.** You heard your sister. Be nice. You have to be nice to me or Mother will get mad as a snake.

*(During the next exchange,* **GERTIE** *climbs onto the chair and switches the enchanted gingerbread with the batch she made.)*

**HANK.** I reckon I can be nice just because I want to.

**BOY.** *(goes to him)* That's dumb. Ain't no one nice just cuz they want to be.

**HANK.** I am. That's how my Mama and Daddy raised me.

**BOY.** What'd they do to you if you weren't nice?

**GIRL.** Did they beat you?

**BOY.** Or lock you in a closet?

**GIRL.** Or threaten to dunk you in milk and eat you all up?

**HANK.** No. They'd just help me remember that we all got feelings and we shouldn't hurt each other's.

**GIRL.** That ain't a fib?

**BOY.** Your Mama and Daddy said that?

**HANK.** They sure did. Mama and Daddy say all kinds of nice things. It's cuz they love us.

**GIRL.** What are they like? Your Mama and Daddy.

**HANK.** Well, they built our little house with their own hands way before Gertie and me was born.

**GIRL.** Is that the house with the shingles?

**HANK.** Yep. And the water pump.

**BOY.** With the blue handle!

**GIRL.** Tell us more.

**HANK.** Well, Mama and Daddy tell the best stories. Daddy makes 'em up and then we all take turns guessin' what the ending's gonna be. It's our favorite game.

**BOY.** It sounds like such fun. *(He notices* **GERTIE** *getting down off the chair.)* Did you get the gingerbread?

**GERTIE.** I considered it, but I reckon maybe you're right. Mother wouldn't like it much if I gave you gingerbread.

**GIRL.** Can you keep a secret?

**GERTIE.** Sure.

**GIRL.** Mother's mean.

**BOY.** She makes us sleep outside and she says she'll tar and feather us if we don't do what she says.

**GERTIE.** That's just awful.

**BOY.** It is awful. I wish we had a Mama and Daddy like you have.

**GERTIE.** Maybe you do, somewhere. Maybe you got lost and trapped, just like we did. Would you like us to help you find your way home?

**GIRL.** To the house with the shingles and the water pump?

**HANK.** Well, that's our house. But we could help you find your house.

**GIRL.** Maybe it's our house, too.

**GERTIE.** How can that be?

**BOY.** I don't know. But I remember it. It's got green shutters.

**GIRL.** And curtains that are yellow, like buttercups.

**GERTIE.** That's our house. How do you know about our house?

*(The* **WITCH** *enters.)*

**WITCH.** Well ain't you just a big happy family?

**GERTIE.** What?

**WITCH.** All my children, here together.

**BOY.** I don't think I'm your child.

**WITCH.** What do you mean by that?

**BOY.** I ain't your child.

**GIRL.** You ain't my mother!

**WITCH.** I think it's time for a little gingerbread. You must be starved. *(She climbs the chair and gets down the gingerbread.)* Here you go – a little piece for each of you. Go on. *(They take it and eat it.)* Now, we'll have no more of that foolish talk.

**BOY.** It ain't foolish. Somethin' ain't right.

**WITCH.** The only thing ain't right is that you didn't eat enough gingerbread. Take some more. *(They eat.)*

**GIRL.** You have to let us go. You ain't my Mother. I have a house of my own, with green shutters.

**WITCH.** This can't be. *(to **GERTIE**)* You! You're awful quiet over there. Cat got your tongue?

**GERTIE.** No, Mother.

**WITCH.** There! That's better. *(to the **GINGERBREAD PEOPLE**)* You two, into the closet with you!

**BOY & GIRL.** No!

**WITCH.** That will teach you to mind me! *(She pushes them into the closet and locks the door.)* Now, Gertie. Did you do your chores this morning?

**GERTIE.** Yes, Mother.

**WITCH.** Did you scrub the floors?

**GERTIE.** Yes, Mother.

**WITCH.** Did you light the oven so I can bake more gingerbread?

**GERTIE.** Yes, Mother.

**WITCH.** Good. *(She open the oven.)* It's just about ready for my secret ingredient.

**GERTIE.** What secret ingredient, Mother?

**WITCH.** It's time you knew, Gertie. I bake very special gingerbread. That's why when you eat it, you do everything I ask, don't you?

**GERTIE.** Of course I do.

**WITCH.** I gave it to your parents, too, and they did everything I asked. They sent you to bed without supper. They led you into the woods and they left you there. Of course, they're giving me a spot of trouble right now, but they won't give me no more once I've made my new batch.

**GERTIE.** They're giving you trouble? Right now?

**WITCH.** Of course, why do you think I had to lock them in the pantry?

**HANK.** Mama! Daddy!

**WITCH.** Shut yer trap, boy! Don't you know how special you are?

**HANK.** What do you mean? How am I special?

**WITCH.** Why, you're the secret ingredient.

**HANK.** What?

**WITCH.** Why do you think I've been feeding you so well? Now that you're nice and plump, I'll bake you into this bread.

**HANK.** And then you can control everyone!

**WITCH.** Well, not everyone. Just the grownups. I've used apple pies and doughnuts – I even used baked potatoes once, but I reckon the gingerbread works better than any of those. I'll have to say thank you to your Daddy. That was a right fine Hansel and Gretel story he made up. I can keep feeding parents gingerbread and they'll lead their little babies right to me. And what better to bring in children than a house made of candy? Now, Gertie! Get your brother out of the cage. *(She hands her the key.)*

**GERTIE.** Yes, Mother. But I ain't sure the oven is quite hot enough yet.

**WITCH.** I'm sure it is – now go get him!

**GERTIE.** But if the oven isn't hot enough, then it won't bake proper and all this time will have been wasted. You'll have to start all over with another little boy. Don't you think you should check first?

**WITCH.** *(opens the oven door)* It feels just fine.

**GERTIE.** But this is a tricky little oven. I noticed that when I was cookin' the stew last week. It feels hot from out here, but it's cool in there.

**WITCH.** *(gets closer)* It still feels hot to me.

**GERTIE.** You might want to get just a little closer. You'll be able to tell so much better when you're right up to it.

**WITCH.** *(sticking her head in the oven)* It's plenty hot from here.

**GERTIE.** Good! *(She pushes the **WITCH** into the oven and slams the door closed.)*

**WITCH.** Let me out! Let me out!

**GERTIE.** Not a chance! You ain't never bakin' little boys into pies or potatoes again!

**WITCH.** *(one long final scream of death)*

**HANK.** Is she gone?

**GERTIE.** I think so.

**HANK.** Then let me out of here!

**GERTIE.** Oh! I'm coming! *(She unlocks the cage. They embrace. There is knocking from the pantry.)*

**MAMA.** Let us out!

**DADDY.** Are you out there?

**GERTIE.** Mama!

**HANK.** Daddy! *(They run to the pantry and open the door.)*

**MAMA.** Hank! Gertie!

**DADDY.** My children!

**GERTIE.** Was it really you all the time?

**MAMA.** We wanted to tell you, but it was like we was lost.

**DADDY.** You found us! We are so proud of you.

**HANK.** Gertie did it. She figured out how to get rid of the witch.

**GERTIE.** We both did.

**MAMA.** Are we ready to go back home?

**HANK.** Do you know the way?

**DADDY.** I can get us back. Ain't nothin' gonna keep me from home again.

**HANK.** We can take some of this food with us. The pantry's almost full.

**MAMA.** I ain't eatin' any more of her food. We don't know what's in it.

**DADDY.** Don't you fret about food, Hank. We'll make due.

**MAMA.** We always have.

**HANK.** Gertie and me, we're old enough to get ourselves jobs now.

**GERTIE.** We don't need to get jobs just yet, Hank.

**HANK.** What do you mean?

**GERTIE.** I found somethin' when I was switching the bread. Wait. *(She climbs up on the chair and gets down a bag. She rattles it. It's full of coins.)* Do you hear that?

**DADDY.** Coins?

**GERTIE.** *(opening the bag)* Gold coins! We can take care of the whole town with this!

**HANK.** Gertie?

**GERTIE.** What is it?

**HANK.** I think we got our happy ending, after all.

*(They embrace)*

**SONG - GRACE (REPRISE)**

**ALL.**
LORD OF THE MOUNTAINS
LORD OF THE TREES
LORD OF THE POSSUMS
AND LORD OF THE BEES
WE GATHER TOGETHER
AT THE END OF THE DAY
TO OFFER THIS BLESSING
TO HIM THAT WE PRAY.
THANK YOU FOR GIVING US
COURAGE TO FIGHT

THANKS FOR THE STRENGTH
TO STAND UP FOR WHAT'S RIGHT
THANKS FOR OUR HOME
AND OUR OWN CROOKED TREE
BUT WE'RE MOST GRATEFUL, LORD
FOR OUR SWEET FAMILY. AMEN.

# Also by
# Kristin Walter...


## The Elves and the Shoemaker


## The Last of the Dragons


## Rapunzel


## The Selfish Giant

# OTHER TITLES AVAILABLE FROM BAKER'S PLAYS

## RAPUNZEL

### Kristin Walter and Michael Walter

*Musical / 2m, 3f / multiple settings*

In this twist on the classic fairy tale, Rapunzel is snatched from her parents on the night of her birth by the evil witch who lives next door and is raised in a tower for sixteen years. The beautiful young woman finds her prince, but he turns out to be quite different than she expected; he is her twin brother! Together, they defeat the witch and are reunited with their true parents.

"In addition to the comedy, children will enjoy Michael Walter's
pop score"
- *The New York Times*

"Michael Walter's tuneful music relays the message of endurance
and love conveyed by (Kristin) Walter's lyrics."
- *Off-Off Broadway Review*